I'm Too Busy

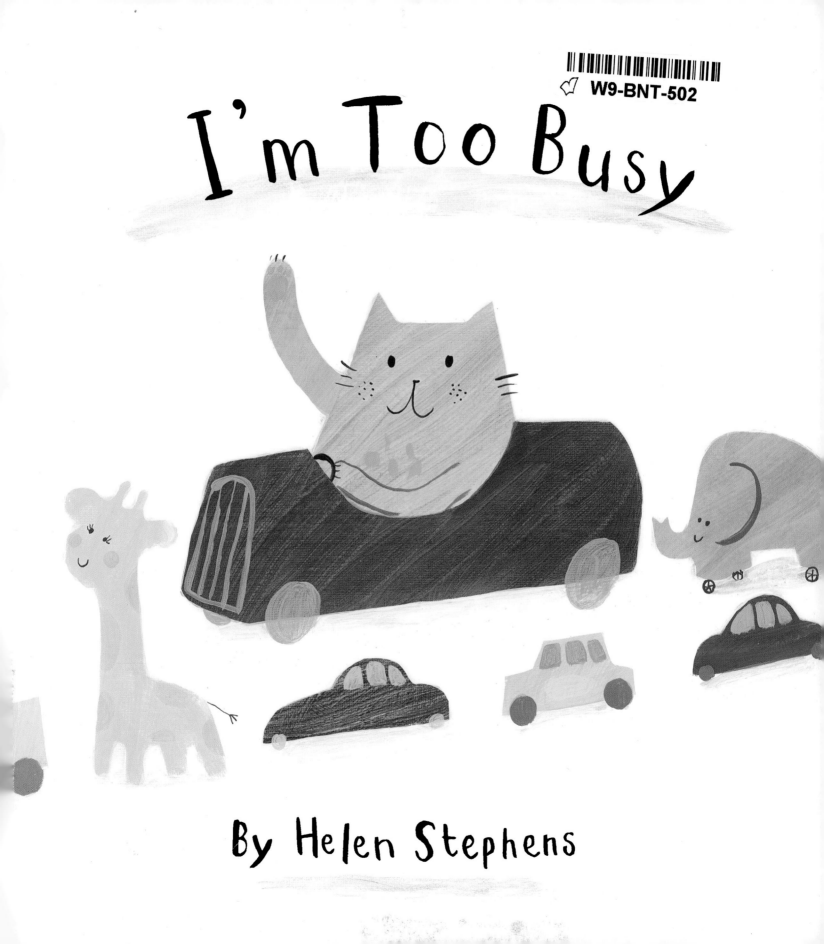

By Helen Stephens

It was a busy day in the city.

Charlie was directing traffic.

"I'm too busy for supper," said Charlie. "I'm directing traffic. Can't you see?"

"Look, Charlie," called Katy, "fish soup!"

"I'm too busy for fish soup,"
said Charlie.
"I'm on the moon.
Can't you see?"

"I've made fish cakes, Charlie," said Katy. "Your favorite."

"Monsters don't eat fish cakes," Charlie growled.

"They eat elephants.
Grrr!"

"There's dessert, too!" called Katy.

"I can see," said Katy, "that you are too busy. Too busy for fish soup, fish cakes, and dessert, too."

Charlie's
tummy
rumbled.

"Fish soup, fish cakes, and **dessert**,"